STARFALL

PHAETON AND THE CHARIOT OF THE SUN

MICHAEL CADNUM

ORCHARD BOOKS ✷ SCHOLASTIC INC.
New York

Library of Congress Cataloging-in-Publication Data is available

0-439-54533-1

10 9 8 7 6 5 4 3 2 1 04 05 06 07 08

Printed in the U.S.A. 37

First Scholastic edition, September 2004

The text type was set in 19-point Post mediaeval.

Book design by Kristina Albertson

for Sherina,
with thanks to Iris

ONE DEER-PRINT

BESIDE

THE SHIVERING POOL

ONE

ONE

THE TWO COUSINS hurried out under the bright late-morning blue, joining the shepherds. Frightened sheep parted around all of them as they dodged the terror from above. Phaeton seized a rock, took aim, and hurled it as hard as he could.

The stone spun upward, and barely missed its target. The griffin banked, still clinging to a bleating lamb. The monster stretched its feathered wings and lashed at the air with its lionlike claws, its dark eyes seeking the source of this fresh attack.

Phaeton heaved another, larger rock – just grazing the griffin's head.

The hairy claws released the lamb, and sent it kicking, sprawling to earth, breathless and gouged but still very much alive. The predator let the afternoon sunlight play along its bronze-bright feathers as it took its time, angling a deliberate circuit around Phaeton. The young man dodged, afraid for his life as the creature dived, its shadow huge and growing larger.

Phaeton fell and rolled, barely escaping the claws.

"Phaeton, let's try for the orchard," piped Cycnus, and the already fleeing shepherds joined in, urging Phaeton to save himself.

"Run, run," mocked the monster.

The youth tumbled again as the talons whistled through the air. The outstretched claws snagged the cloth of Phaeton's *chiton* – his woolen tunic. And held him, straining the fabric, tugging the young man off the ground.

Phaeton struggled, his legs wheeling in midair.

Off-balance, the raptor tried to circle higher, carrying the youth for a few sweeping strokes of its powerful wings – but the fabric tore.

Phaeton tumbled to the ground. When he found his feet again he gave a burst of speed, zigzagging across the meadow.

Cycnus and the shepherds scurried ahead, until the thickly blossomed orchard sheltered all of them.

The griffin gave a roar of frustration, and seized the topmost branches, twigs and petals raining, trying to work his way downward, to reach his human prey.

Phaeton did not linger long with the shepherds, crouching under the trees.

His sandaled feet and his bare legs were a blur, his tunic flowing, apple branches catching at his sleeves.

His lungs began to burn, his vision swam, but fifteen-year-old Phaeton used the power he had been born with, the speed that was his from earliest boyhood. He raced all the way through the orchard, sprinting down into the village of shepherd huts, toward the handsome villa at the center of the settlement, Phaeton's home.

Cycnus ran, too, trailing his long-legged cousin, but soon the youth had to break his stride.

Cycnus gazed after the path Phaeton had taken, blossoms still shivering where he had brushed past.

Cycnus was an orphan, the son of Phaeton's maternal uncle, and he was as close as a younger brother to his active cousin. Cycnus thought of himself as blessed by the fates to have such a safe and happy home. At times like this, however, he knew that it would always lie beyond his power to keep up with Phaeton, whose very name meant *Shining One*.

Phaeton had just enough breath to call a warning as he flung open the gates, startling the servants.

His mother Clymene rose from the shade near the fountain.

"Our flock is being attacked!" he panted.

The house servants gaped, wide-eyed. A soft-voiced, prayerful lot, they knew nothing of rough life under the sky.

Phaeton steadied his voice and spoke formally now, as was proper in the presence of servants. Bad tidings had to be expressed in a careful way, the words chosen deliberately, and the youth steadied his voice.

"Mother," he said at last, "send word to your husband, before the griffin does real harm."

TWO

CLYMENE LOVED her husband Merops for his generosity.

And she loved his house. The fountain here played night and day, and a peacock strode among the herb shrubs of the sun-splashed courtyard, lording harmlessly over the doves that gathered to drink and bathe.

The main house of a wealthy farming estate was usually, like this one, composed of wide walls that enclosed a central refuge, and many women lived as Phaeton's mother chose to do, staying in the quiet confines of the home.

But Clymene was more retiring than most, and all the countryside shared the story that explained her special need for peace and shadow – although not everyone agreed that this tale was true.

In the years of her maidenhood, the summer she had coaxed her father into letting her scamper with the rabbit hunters, the story went, she had found a lover beyond a clump of alder trees.

This lover was none other than Phoebus Apollo – the god of the sun.

She had understood as this handsome presence swept her into his embrace that he would not linger – that he would depart to his duty beyond the gates of sunset. The lord of daylight could blaze up like noon heat, and he could soothe like a warm dawn. But he could not be won, or bound by promises, like a mortal lover.

But she had believed that she found a special favor in his eyes – that of all the women under the blue he loved her best.

So she had believed.

He called her *alma* – dear one. She had swelled with child in the following months, her prayers to the morning sun unanswered. Summer ripened to harvest time all those years ago, and the lovely Clymene learned to relish solitude, and the laughter of her infant son. The beautiful young woman told herself that she did not regret her lover's absence, and that her heart was free of longing.

After a few summers the wealthy Merops adopted the boy Phaeton as his own, gracing Clymene with marriage vows. Her wedding had been a joyous feast, still remembered in the farmland, with the finest meats and wines, and golden acorns and hazelnuts strewn on the ground for good luck.

Merops was a kind husband, careful with every living creature he owned. If a barrow-pig lost a tusk, or a pigeon sprained a wing, Merops hurried off to attend to the injured creature. Clymene loved him for his kindness and for his quiet laugh.

Even so, Merops was a mortal man, and not the god of daylight. Clymene wondered sometimes if Phaeton's father ever savored the sight of the lad at play, from his chariot across the noontime blue. She avoided bright sunlight increasingly in recent summers, keeping to the shade. Let my son's father be teased with curiosity, she thought, and forever wonder. Let him ache for a glimpse of me, as I once did pine for him.

Of all that she enjoyed now she treasured nothing so much as the sight of her son. When a beesting had nearly taken his life a few summers ago, her sacred locket – with the knucklebone of a sea hero – had worked magic, but Clymene felt her son should be spared such dangers.

The sound of his step, the murmur of his voice, always quickened her heart. Now she was alarmed at his sudden news.

"How many men has the griffin killed?" she asked with an air of calm.

"No one, while I was there," said her son.

No woman who had been intimate with a god was easily disturbed. She had been afraid some ancient Titan had stirred to life – a raving giant – or some equal horror. Griffins were like so much else in the woodlands and hills – spiteful toward human beings, and envious of the love men and women could share for each other.

Nonetheless, Clymene resented the threat her son had just encountered. Surely Apollo could extend some special protection to the youth. Besides, she was proud of the sort of young man Phaeton was turning out to be. The son of Phoebus Apollo did certainly resemble his father – with his honey-bright hair and his sky-bright eye.

And she was more concerned than she wanted Phaeton to see, despite her pretense. His shoulders bore flecks of tree bark, and an oak leaf was caught in his hair. She plucked it free and said, "You haven't been near the Nymph Tree, Phaeton, have you?"

Clymene had heard Phaeton and Cycnus planning a gift of honeycomb for Ino, but never guessed the danger her son was willing to risk. Someone should take an ax to that old oak, she thought – it festered with bees. Or better yet, the immortal god of sunlight should parch it with his rays and kill the tree, and all the winged insects, too.

"Tell me, dear Phaeton," insisted Clymene, "that you have not climbed that old oak to find honeycomb for Ino."

"Don't – please don't worry about me, Mother," stammered Phaeton.

He was more than a little embarrassed. His mother must have overheard Cycnus urging caution, and Phaeton insisting that surely the long-haired Ino, daughter of the local river merchant, would be impressed with such a gift.

Affection warmed Phaeton's eyes, but his voice was impatient when he added, "Send for Merops, Mother, please – before the griffin kills every living thing."

THREE

PHAETON'S STEPFATHER hurried toward them at that moment, rolling up the scroll in his hand, an inventory of wheat bushels and breed-ewes, an estimate of the bountiful harvest to come.

Hearing the news, Merops asked at once, "Where is Cycnus?"

"I left him safe," said Phaeton, realizing he had not given his cousin much thought, "in the apple orchard, I think."

"Dear goddess of love," breathed Merops, "I'm grateful for that."

It was not the first time that the young man had felt impatience at his stepfather's character. When confronted with bad news most men gave out a manly "by Hercules!" But quiet Merops whispered a prayer to the goddess Venus, like a philosopher.

Now Phaeton wondered as before why his mother hadn't married a tough, sun-weathered adventurer with a hearty laugh – like the traders who bought horses from Merops early each summer, stallions bound for chariot duty in the far reaches of the world.

And so Phaeton's heart leaped when Merops called for the farm-steward, and gave the command, "Arm the workers with scythes and axes."

And Phaeton was glad to hear his stepfather add, "We'll teach this griffin a lesson he won't forget."

Phaeton was proud of the sturdy band of servants and neighbors that marched quickly across the village square, brandishing scythes, boar spears, and cattle prods.

Old Aristander had donned one of his time-honored helmets, from the days when he crafted armor for sea traders and fought alongside them. The stout bronzesmith still fastened the fittings of his crocodile-skin armor as he outpaced all but Phaeton.

The veteran smiled at the young man and said, "We'll cut out this monster's gizzard, Phaeton, and have a tasty feast!"

The young man did not want to say what he was thinking, even as the old campaigner lifted his *pelta* – a crescent-shaped shield: Be careful, honored Aristander – your best fighting days are past.

Phaeton's youthful half sisters joined them, long-limbed Phaethusa, nearly as fleet of foot as her brother, and Lampetia, who made birds and beasts out of red river clay.

Phaeton lifted a gentle hand to stay them. The anticipated violence was too dangerous for the very young, and Merops agreed, "Stay here in the village and guard the threshing ground," said their kind-eyed father.

"Phaeton, bring me back a feather," called Lampetia. "Please!"

Her half brother laughed and waved, wondering inwardly that his sisters knew so little of danger.

The band was a brave sight, Phaeton knew, and when Ino called out from the wellhead, where she helped one of her servant girls crank water out of the ground, Phaeton gave a wave.

"There's trouble in the sheep field," was all he would allow himself to say, imitating the terseness of warriors who had seen much violence.

"Phaeton, be careful!" called Ino, hurrying to join him.

The young woman had rarely spoken like this to Phaeton. They played drafts together, a board game with ivory pieces, and sometimes she sang for him, poems Phaeton had barely heard of, learned from ambassadors and river captains.

Some day he would write a song of his own, or memorize an epic, some artful way to prove his worth to her. But for now he could not trust himself to say anything further. Something about her struck him speechless, as so often before.

Phaeton was pleased to note, however, that the golden-haired young woman followed along, accepting a hunting lance from one of the field workers as the band stormed through the orchard, ready to battle the monster.

Perhaps, thought Phaeton, I'll seize the griffin, and wound it somehow – as Ino watches.

FOUR

THE THRONG of armed villagers hurried into the meadow.

They were just in time to see young Epaphus, bending his bow, taking aim at his winged quarry.

The feathered monster let out a wordless, piercing challenge just as an arrow lanced into the sky. The arrow caught the sunlight, glinting as it arced upward. The griffin tried to time its flight to avoid this menace – and it succeeded, fluttering its great wings.

But a second bolt immediately followed the first.

This new shaft buried itself in the griffin's throat, and the creature let out a breathy scream. The monster wheeled awkwardly, trailing feathers. It struggled to remain aloft, but at last plunged downward, unable to break its fall, and landed hard on the grassy field.

"Come see!" called Epaphus, brandishing the bow, a bristling quiver of arrows at his hip.

He gave his chest a pat. *Come see what I've just done.*

The young hunter propped one booted foot on the flank of the bloody, barely moving griffin as the villagers gathered around, giving cries of congratulations and thanksgiving.

The arrow thrust from the throat of the monster, where the eagle-like plumage of the head and neck mingled with the tawny, lionlike body. The creature's eyes were half-open, a black tongue darting from its metallic beak.

The griffin snapped at the air, and Phaeton joined others in taking a step back. As much as he hated and feared the creature, it gave the young man no pleasure to see it suffer.

Epaphus gave Phaeton a bold glance and laughed.

"While one of our neighbors ran as fast as he was able," said the young archer, "another planted his feet and bent his bow."

"Well done, Epaphus," said Merops. He put his hand on the suntanned hunter's shoulder.

"Oh, very well indeed, Epaphus!" sang out Ino.

Phaeton was fleet of foot, and he knew how to ride a spirited horse. But he had no training in the art of archery – it was not considered a seemly skill for the stepson of a gentleman. Now as so often before Phaeton bitterly resented his stepfather's quiet household, with its thoughtful-looking marble ancestors lined up in the hall. His father should be a war hero, his walls lined with battle trophies.

"And thanks to quick-footed Phaeton, too," said Merops, "for alerting us to danger."

The gathered folk gave a cheer for both young men.

A youth less blinded by feeling would have seen that Merops was merely proper toward the prideful archer, but that he reserved a warm smile for his stepson. And he would have seen that Ino, while dazzled by Epaphus's prowess, put her hand to her throat, dismayed at the way the young hunter kicked the dying griffin, and kicked again, causing the creature further agony.

When he kicked the monster once more the black beak parted, and released an airy groan. The griffin's head fell back into the dust, but even now the beast was not dead, panting, red eyes searching. A more merciful hunter would use a knife, now, to bring this suffering to an end.

Ino turned away, but Epaphus for the moment had no eyes for her.

"Apollo is the god of the bow and arrow," continued Epaphus, "as everyone knows."

"Phoebus Apollo in his chariot admires archery," admitted Old Aristander, his voice muffled by the helmet he loved to wear, "almost as much as he approves a good song."

"So, Phaeton," said Epaphus, radiant in the bright noon. "I've heard you bragging about your divine father."

Phaeton had mentioned his parentage in quiet moments, believing his mother's word. Now he regretted ever opening his mouth around the young hunter.

"Tell me truthfully now, Phaeton," Epaphus was continuing, "who among us is the son of a god? A mild-hearted dreamer?"

Phaeton seethed inwardly. The young archer was blessed with a rooster's voice as well as an archer's eye. Besides, good-humored tradition allowed a successful hunter, like a victorious athlete, to boast of his triumph.

But the sound of Epaphus's voice stung Phaeton, as the archer added, "Or somone like me?" He laughed and continued, "Phaeton, you have to admit it's possible. Maybe I'm the offspring of Jupiter himself!"

FIVE

IF PHAETON could have thought of any smart rejoinder, he would have uttered it right then.

But instead he said nothing. He knelt to gather a single gilt-red feather from the ground, remembering Lampetia's request.

"Phaeton, everyone knows you're just another wool comber," continued Epaphus, using the phrase for a housebound man of little adventure. "And the offspring of a peddler, or maybe a wandering goatherd." At that, the young hunter drew his knife, and cut the griffin's throat.

The assembly of field hands and house servants fell silent at the insult they had heard. Only Merops's habitual even temper kept him from striking the young archer – this offense to Clymene and her son was beyond bad manners. Even so, the good-tempered landowner grew stiff and pale.

Show none of your troubled pride, Phaeton cautioned himself. *Dignity answers the jeer.* It was a line from an old fable, the hard-laboring ant mocked by the lounging grasshopper. It was true that a quiet reserve was admired by man and god alike.

The veteran Aristander shifted the heavy helmet back from his face and offered, in a halting effort to soothe, "Certainly, my friends, both lads may be the sons of one god or another."

This suggestion merely embittered Phaeton all the more.

Epaphus, alerted by the silence of his former well-wishers, now a disapproving circle of villagers, may have begun to stammer an apology.

But Phaeton did not linger to hear it.

He made his way with a measured tread toward home with Cycnus beside him offering consolation, "That loutish archer will only offend the gods, Phaeton."

As always Cycnus made good sense, Phaeton knew. He was grateful to his bright-haired cousin, who could recite many legends about the gods and their exploits. But for the moment Phaeton could not be consoled by talk.

Phaeton broke from his loyal cousin and ran.

He took solace, as so often before, in the sound of the wind streaming through his hair.

Once again Phaeton flung open the gate of his stepfather's villa and quickly entered the courtyard.

Clymene was there, embroidering the hem of a cloth.

The soft-spun, woolen garment belonged to her son. She was sewing green and gold thread along the hem of his favorite tunic, preparing for the celebration of summer, yet weeks away, a festival of dancing and the best reserves of wine.

Clymene paused, her needle glinting in the light reflected off the water of the fountain. She gave a nod and a worried smile, and her servants departed, their soft steps fading to silence.

Phaeton did not speak at once.

He did not want to awaken a hurtful secret from his mother's past. If anything, a protective instinct for her heart, as well as his own, had silenced Phaeton for many seasons. Even now he weighed his question and silently asked the Mother of Wisdom, gray-eyed Minerva, to guide his speech.

But even with all the consideration he managed to give his words, they came out sounding harsh.

"Promise me before the gods, Mother," insisted Phaeton, "that I am the son of the lord of daylight."

SIX

PHAETON'S TONE was rough, despite his intentions, and almost unseemly – a son's address to his mother should always be polite.

But Clymene was a woman slow to anger. She was aware that she had offered her growing son too much silence on this long-unspoken question, and that she had stifled her own memories too long.

Only a careful eye would have noticed the needle trembling, her quickened pulse alive in the green and golden thread. Clymene slipped the needle safely into the garment on her lap.

Strong feeling stirring in her voice she asked, "Who has dared to say otherwise?"

Phaeton had always, until this moment, taken pleasure in this courtyard.

Like many children, he had formed soldiers of potter's clay, shaved by friendly potters from their turning wheels. Baked in the sun, these warriors had played out their triumphs here beside the dancing waters.

Now the young man reported Epaphus's insult, regretting even as he spoke that he had troubled his mother this day, disturbing Clymene – but bringing him closer to the inevitable and disappointing truth.

When Phaeton concluded the news of his young adversary and the defeated griffin, Clymene plucked the silver thimble from her finger, and tossed it onto the bricks.

"Epaphus's mother is that mouse-haired creature, Thalia," she said angrily, "who noised it about the village that I was the companion of ox-herders and wine-sots, little better than herself."

The noblewoman hesitated, displeased at her own outburst. She continued in a more gentle cadence, "The gods have other consorts among mortal women, Phaeton my son, but none of them make this countryside their home."

"I doubt that it is possible," said Phaeton. He had long ago come to question such matters, and now he could not keep silent. "Forgive me, Mother, but I certainly can't believe that the god of sunlight seeks the love of mortal women like yourself."

Phaeton at once wished he had not said this – but it was too late. He had spoken, and now his mother knew how he felt.

Clymene folded her hands and wished the divinities of the hearth could grant her the proper response to this. She gazed up from her shadowy seat toward the sunlight, still falling this late in the afternoon, golden across the fountain.

No god, she believed, should abandon his son to face both a griffin and a common insult in one day. And certainly no deity should allow his offspring to doubt the loving power of the gods.

Even with an effort to speak formally, Phaeton's voice trembled as he added, "I now understand the true nature of my parentage, and on the subject I will never pain you again."

"You do not trouble me, Phaeton," said the gentlewoman. *Your divine father troubles me*, she nearly allowed herself to add.

The young man spoke with difficulty, but with the added dignity divine Minerva graced him with that hour. "I imagine now that my father was some mortal man you cannot bring yourself to mention."

Clymene felt years of consolation fall away before her. Knowing the truth, and believing that Phaeton shared it, had kept her heart alive during the long and bitter winter nights.

"Can you so doubt me, Phaeton?" she asked.

Phaeton turned away.

Clymene rose, and she stepped into the bold sunlight she had avoided for too long.

She took her son by the hand and turned to look upward at that source of light so rich it is blinding. She closed her eyes and felt the radiance gather her in, flooding her, her senses alight.

"I swear under the Lightning-Thruster's blue sky," she said, beginning the most solemn of oaths, one uttered before Jupiter. She raised her voice, "I swear upon the life of the husband I love that your father was the divine Phoebus."

This oath shook Phaeton deeply.

And it awakened the beginnings of joy.

Then, stirred by some inner daemon, or by Venus herself, the bringer of desire, Clymene turned to her son and continued, "Go to him, Phaeton."

The young man blinked his eyes, his gaze tearful from gazing upward, and bewildered, too, at his mother's meaning.

"It is not right," said Clymene, "that you face dangers and even churlish insult without your driving father's help."

Phaeton held up his hand to shade his eyes from the all-searching sun.

"Take yourself," his mother was saying, "to the end of the world, all the way to the gates of sunrise and seek your father in his temple."

"Is such a journey possible?" asked Phaeton, his voice a bare whisper.

But he was thrilled, nonetheless – everything he had ever doubted was suddenly made certain.

"Leave today," said Clymene, "and let your immortal father tell you all about his love for a fleet-footed maiden."

SEVEN

IN THE WARMTH of the slanting afternoon sunlight that very day, Phaeton called out his farewells.

His half sisters Lampetia and Phaethusa joined their voices in a parting-hymn to Mercury, most famous of all divine messengers, herald to the gods, and guardian of travelers. His youngest sister held up the single, sun-gilded griffin feather as she joined with the others:

Lighten each footfall,
quicken each prayer
from our lips to heaven.

Merops lifted his hand in blessing, his prayerful formality unable to hide the tears in his eyes.

Told of the trek Clymene had urged on her son, gentlehearted Merops had only sighed, "Dear Phaeton, alas!" As head of the household the nobleman could have forbidden Phaeton's journey, but knowing Clymene's heart, and loving his stepson, the soft-voiced landowner had endowed Phaeton with a satchel of provisions and, secure in the heel of the sack, a small bag of silver.

Merops would not admit as much, but he had always been slightly in awe of Clymene – she had once, after all, been the consort of a god. While it was a thrill to be the husband of such a woman, he had always been reluctant to differ with her on whether the new cook had overboiled the groats, or if raisin wine was good enough for a midwinter meal. He had been more than gentle, likewise, with her son, not wishing to displease the offspring of a divinity, even though his nature never permitted harsh speech toward any of his children.

Clymene looked on, her eyes alive with faith in Phaeton's journey, but afraid to make a sound lest she give way to weeping. She would miss her son with every heartbeat, but she knew his pilgrimage would win him honor – and her, as well.

And Phaeton's journey would forever silence Thalia, that queen of gossip.

Phaeton could not guess what song or prayer Ino was lifting, her voice lost among the others, but he took a long moment to gaze back at her.

The beginning of a journey was very important. It was then that bird-omens were made visible. If a thrush or a swallow flew a straight course in the direction of one's destination it was a very favorable sign. A crooked flight – or even worse, one heading back in the direction of home – foretold hardship.

But Phaeton could see no birds at all as he passed the still-smoking smithy and the abode of Old Aristander, who called out his best wishes.

The young man's sole omen was his own enigmatic shadow, falling ahead on the stones and ruts of the road.

Ino put her fingers wonderingly to her lips.

"Is he going off, then," Ino heard herself ask, "just like that – without a further farewell?"

In his sorrow at his cousin's departure, Cycnus felt a spark of jealousy. "Ino, do you really think," said the youth, "that Phaeton should stay a little longer – simply to share sweet good-byes with you?"

Ino realized now how little she had guessed about Phaeton.

"It would not displease me," she said. She added, "I would have been very happy if he had –"

Kissed me. To her surprise those words had been on her lips.

Cycnus ran off, believing that it was not too late to speak to Phaeton again.

He hurried, as he so often had seen Phaeton run, ducking the branches of the fruit trees, eager to do some wonderful deed to prove his friendship and loyalty.

Perhaps the only silent, dry-eyed figure in the village was Epaphus, standing with his bow unstrung.

The young archer was able to guess the motive behind Phaeton's journey, and for this reason Phaeton's rival was a knot of self-doubt. If a god sired me, the young hunter thought, shouldn't I set forth on a journey, too?

He had many questions to ask his mother.

Armed with his staff, and carrying a satchel of wheat cakes and *pemma* – finest pastry – and apples still cold from the cellar, Phaeton made quick work of passing the vineyards.

He bid a silent farewell to the herds of cattle, lowing animals trailing in to be milked. Long strides swept him through the fields of rippling wheat to the edge of the wild land. A row of stones there, mossy-furred boulders, marked the outline of the woods. Some said these rocks had once been men and women, transformed by some wondrous power.

Phaeton hurried past them. Sometimes, he had heard, these human-sized stones were heard to murmur strange, barely audible warnings or pleas for life.

The young seeker reached a ragged crossroads.

The way ahead was well traveled, worn bare by oxcarts and wandering magi, men from the east who read the future in the stars. Few people from the countryside journeyed beyond this crossroads, a departure place marked by a statue of Mercury to bring good luck.

Night was already rising all around, stars just beginning to prick the first-dark.

As darkness was nearly complete, footsteps came from behind.

A breathless voice called his name.

EIGHT

CYCNUS HURRIED through the cropland in the light of the setting sun, and fell wordlessly to one knee. He held out a woven grass basket.

Phaeton parted the cleverly-knit parcel, and brought forth a shining, beautifully wrought amulet.

"Brave Cycnus!" said Phaeton, touched deeply. "Thank you, cousin – but I cannot accept this!"

It was a magical amulet featuring the face of the legendary Gorgon – her tongue distended, her hair a mass of writhing snakes. Many people wore such amulets to ward off evil. This was an especially valuable image, an heirloom of heavy silver, a gift to Cycnus from his dying father.

"If it brings you safely back again, Phaeton," said the youthful cousin, "I will part with it gladly."

Phaeton was surprised at the feeling that stirred in him now, one that even made him take a faltering step back toward home. He had hoped, only half-aware of the impulse, that Cycnus had arrived to tell Phaeton that Clymene had relented, and that a general outcry demanded Phaeton's immediate return.

"I might lose this honored treasure, cousin," Phaeton was saying.

"Then take me with you," said Cycnus hopefully, "to keep it and you both entirely safe."

Phaeton returned the precious amulet to his cousin's hands with a regretful smile.

"Never laugh at any of Epaphus's jokes," cautioned Phaeton with a mock frown, "until I come home again."

"I would sooner a pair of ass's ears sprouted from my head," said Cycnus.

"And let Ino wear this amulet," Phaeton added, "if she walks out to the sheep meadow." It was believed that griffins bred for life, like wild geese. A mournful griffin might well seek revenge against the villagers.

"Tell her," added Phaeton, "that I'm about to do something wonderful."

"Oh, Phaeton," asked Cycnus excitedly, "tell me – what will it be?"

TWO

WHAT WILL IT BE?

Cycnus's question echoed in Phaeton's mind as daylight entirely ebbed, and the young man traveled eastward along the path alone.

Already the road was less worn, with fewer hoofprints and wheel ruts.

The dark sky was growing rich with stars, this wealth of light forming the shapes of animals in the heavens. Aries the ram sparkled in the vault of darkness, along with Taurus the bull, and the crab and the lion. Far to the south coiled the likeness of a scorpion.

Some said that these points of light were all that was visible of actual, gigantic beings, able to stir and strike. Phaeton did not quite believe that this was true – but he did not know for certain.

Moving cautiously in the dark wood, he bedded by a spring, the pool welling from the earth and flowing through thick grasses.

In his weariness, and with the homesickness that already nagged him, he did not feel much anxiety about lying down in this unfamiliar forest.

No human outlaws haunted such bramble-thick wild woods, he believed. Certainly no youthful wayfarer would have dared, either – except this one particular seeker hoping that lordly Apollo and the divine Mercury themselves had already blessed his journey.

Phaeton's sleep was fitful.

Many times he woke during the night to wonder at the sound of wind in the trees, or splashing in the spring waters, and even the sound of stealthy whispering nearby. He took his stout staff into his hand.

I'll stay awake – no matter what.

But he only sat up blinking later in the night, shaking off sleep once again, aware that someone – or some uncanny creature – had said something in his ear.

His sleep was broken by birdsong, too, the low-voiced owl and the liquid trill of the *aedon* – the nightingale.

In the first gray dawn, Phaeton abandoned all hope of getting rest and crept to the living waters of the spring. He knelt and drank from his cupped hands.

He started and sprang to his feet.

A hand had reached up from the depths to touch his lips – and then darted quickly, back into the shallows.

Phaeton would have fled at that moment, through the tangle of saplings, and out to the footpath.

What kept him there, though, was the knowledge of nymph-lore he had heard from his earliest childhood, stories of magical creatures of surpassing beauty. Phaeton knew the danger – Old Aristander was rumored to have spent a night wandering half-mad years ago as a result of a single kiss from a *dryad* – a wood nymph.

"I mean you no harm," the young man heard his own voice say.

An as yet shapeless vision drifted upward from the spring, paused for a long moment, and then fell away again.

"I swear by the divine Diana," said Phaeton, even more boldly, "that I am a friend."

The indistinct shape reappeared and continued its halting climb toward the light. And sank again. Only to rise higher within a few heartbeats, closer to the morning daylight.

At last this apparition kissed the surface of the water, sending forth a pulsing, widening circle.

And at once shrank back again.

While uneasy, Phaeton was at the same time extremely pleased. Few mortal youths could claim an encounter with such a wonder.

"Good day to you!" he said.

Perhaps he spoke too loudly. The creature vanished entirely, now, back into the abyss, but not before Phaeton had glimpsed a being of cunning beauty.

Since boyhood Phaeton had heard that these *naiads* – water nymphs – kept palaces in the deeps, and that while they were not immortal they lived for thousands of years.

Emboldened by the apparent shyness of this water-creature the young man allowed himself to offer, "I am called Phaeton."

Against the whisper of the busy waters his name did not sound very impressive.

Perhaps this was why the young traveler did not hesitate to continue, saying, "I am known as Phaeton, the son of Phoebus on high." He offered this in what he thought was an unboastful manner.

Without any further warning this keen-eyed being's face was at the water's edge, very close to the young man's feet – too close. Now it was Phaeton's turn to fall back in alarm.

The naiad studied him, her long dark hair streaming back from her glowing features.

Such nymphs were believed to be the daughters of Jupiter, and while not hostile to human hopes, they were felt to be beyond mortal understanding.

Phaeton spoke again. "I am on my way to visit my divine father, beyond the gates of dawn."

At that the pale shape darted forward, seized Phaeton's satchel of fruit and wheat cakes, and vanished into the water. Phaeton called out and scrambled down to the thick grasses at the water's edge.

Too late.

He reached into the bubbling waters of the spring, but at once a grasp had him, encircling his wrist. Torn between the urge to escape, and an enduring fascination with this woodland creature, Phaeton tried to withdraw his hand – but he couldn't.

Alarmed, as he rapidly became, the youth could remember no charm or invocation that could help him, and could only flail, yelling for any divine power in this place to help free an innocent traveler.

Just as quickly as it had seized him, the unseen hand released Phaeton.

TEN

THE PATH through the woods was a lattice of daylight and shadow.

Some people have lively blood, and feeling shows quickly in their features. Phaeton was one of these, and he blushed now as he murmured to himself, "What a blessing that Ino will never hear of this!"

He hurried along with his staff – but without his provisions. You have no food, now, and no silver, Phaeton could imagine

Merops and Clymene scolding him – and it's a wonder you weren't drowned.

Or kissed – and driven mad.

The young seeker saw only one other human being that troubled morning, a man garbed in a *pellis* – a tunic of animal skins – gathering wild carrots. Such folk lived in scattered huts, making their way to villages on market day, and, being neither slaves nor servants, were often proud of their freedom.

"Tell me, friend, what creatures dwell within these woods?" Phaeton inquired politely, hoping to hear that nothing more dangerous than a woodpecker lived here.

The woodsman said nothing. He groped for his wooden-bladed shovel, holding the tool as a weapon, ready to strike. Sometimes, a magical and potentially dangerous being took on the disguise of a mortal, and no one could be too careful.

"I'd be grateful, good freedman," added Phaeton in a tone of high courtesy, "for a bite of carrot or parsnip."

The root gatherer took a deep breath and relaxed his grip on the shovel. Phaeton's request proved that he was most likely human. Gods fed on *ambrosia* – a sweet nourishment unknown among men, and a daemon – a spirit-being – could not be said to eat at all.

Phaeton wiped the mud from the offered carrot with a fern leaf, and chewed the sun-gold root gratefully.

"All manner of beasts, young traveler," said the woodsman, not unkindly, "hide in these forests."

"I am very sorry to hear it," said the young man earnestly.

"Speak to none of them," added the woodsman. "And see that you especially avoid that band of wandering centaurs."

Phaeton's heart sank. "Surely there aren't many of those terrible horse-men around?"

The root-gatherer raised a finger and sniffed the air. "I can smell them," he said, "at a thousand paces."

Phaeton inhaled deeply, but to his senses the air was flavored only with leaf-mold and earth, and a hint of flowering myrtle.

When the young man turned to thank the woodsman he had vanished.

Spring flowers brushed the hem of the young adventurer's woolen tunic as he hurried ahead, grateful for the splashing sunlight that gleamed on the flowering berry bushes and the wings of birds. The single carrot had done little more than stir the youth's hunger.

Such hunger is a nagging misfortune, and with each step Phaeton grew all the more famished. And his hunger was not his sole concern.

A large figure shadowed Phaeton's progress, off in the nearby evergreens. This strange four-legged beast was certainly not another nymph, and surely not a man. This beast was, furthermore, too big to be a satyr – one of the goat-men who molested travelers, especially unprotected women.

It was, in truth, a hooved creature, strongly muscled, and steadily following Phaeton through the forest.

Phaeton swung the staff experimentally, wondering if it would make a stout weapon.

More hoofbeats echoed through the woods.

Phaeton bounded, faster than he had ever run before.

ELEVEN

THE SOUND of approaching hooves crunched through the undergrowth, an easy, loping gallop, keeping pace with Phaeton's fleetest efforts.

He was aware that he was not being pursued so much as followed. The young man ran hard, the wind whistling in his ears, overhanging trees snatching at his clothes, until it seemed that he would surely succeed in leaving the centaurs behind.

But the thud of the hooves stayed close – growing closer.

Breathing hard, the young seeker came to a muddy crossroads, a weathered head of Mercury marking the site. Even here in the wild, Phaeton was grateful to see, images of the divine messenger watched over a traveler's journey.

The shrine was moss-freckled, green with neglect and weather. "Wing-footed immortal," Phaeton began praying breathlessly, *lighten my footsteps, quicken my prayer –*

But in his alarm Phaeton could not finish his devotions. The sound of hooves was even louder, and as the young man hurried forward, a herd of horselike creatures, half-hidden by the woods, closed in around him.

Sometimes, in summers past, Phaeton and Cycnus had pretended to be Hercules, battling an attack of such horselike creatures, defending a wedding or a festival from the ruthless half-men. On such afternoons the boyish Phaeton had played at being such a monster, stamping and scowling.

But the young son of Clymene had never actually seen such a beast before, a centaur with a tangled beard cantering, circling the young traveler, blocking his path. The four-hooved, half-man gripped a bloody club – or was it a human limb? – in his right fist.

He's not so fierce-looking, Phaeton tried to reassure himself. He looks smaller than you'd expect – and much advanced in years, however strongly built.

Phaeton lifted a clear-voiced greeting, as good manners required, wishing the centaur the gods' blessing on such a morning.

The centaur was eating with a show of carelessness, gnawing on what now appeared to be the shank of an animal – a deer, Phaeton guessed hopefully.

At last the gray-bearded creature tossed the bloody limb off into the woods and wiped his mouth on the back of his hand. His muscular haunches splashed a puddle, and the creature took a few half-steps to find solid footing, eyeing Phaeton all the while.

Several more centaurs had gathered, half-hidden by the boughs of trees until they paced into the sunlight. While none of them were armed with spears or clubs, one or two carried silver drinking horns, and a bald-headed centaur to the rear of the herd picked up a branch, hefted it, and began to peel it of leaves.

Some said that these horse-men were the offspring of the primitive gods, the Titans who ruled earth before the Olympic divinities and, some believed, still sprawled sleeping among the mountains. Phaeton had heard stories about a legendary centaur called Chiron, who was king of a breed of such creatures, and wise enough to teach the children of men.

For this reason the young traveler sensed that further human speech would not be entirely wasted on them. He spoke clearly, addressing the centaurs with a wish for their good health, and adding, "I am Phaeton, the son of Apollo."

The bearded centaur lifted a hind hoof and scratched his flank. He flicked his tail in an easy circle, giving no sign of having understood the young man's assertion.

"Phoebus Apollo," said Phaeton, indicating the morning sun spilling through the trees above, "is my father."

The centaur stretched, patted his belly, and gave a long, loud belch.

They were not so fierce after all, Phaeton thought. Their horselike portions were more like hunting ponies than war mounts. Their manlike arms and shoulders were well developed, but no more than those of bricklayers or plowmen. Besides, these manbeasts had a rank odor that drew flies, the insects arriving through the morning light.

The young man felt the first stirrings of confidence – and exasperation.

"My father," he said slowly and clearly, one hand on his breast, "is the sun on high, who watches all the earth from his chariot." He pointed upward, then indicated the woodland all around.

The others drew even closer, mud-and-manure-grimed creatures, the heat from their horselike bodies enclosing the young man, their stink like the foulest of stables left to ferment.

The bloody-handed centaur, his jaws busy with some gristly scrap, at last spat and gave a grunt. To Phaeton's relief, the centaur began to speak.

He used a dialect from the mountain regions far to the north, where centaurs had long ago originated.

"Did you hear him say that he has a name?" said the bloody-handed creature, consulting his fellows. "And that he has a father?"

"Yes, we understood him well enough," said one. This youthful-looking centaur gave a laugh, and reached down to pluck a stone from the road – a big, round stone. He tossed this rock easily in his hands.

The bloody-handed, gray-bearded centaur then leaned close – Phaeton could smell his carrion breath. "Have you any wine?"

"As you see, I carry nothing," Phaeton was quick to respond.

Centaurs were by reputation often driven mad by the least whiff of strong drink, and centaurs who had swallowed so much as a half cup grew violent and lustful.

"No wine," said the centaur in a tone of regret.

"You can see that for yourself," said Phaeton, his spirits rising. "I carry no food or drink. But I'll take away with me your reputation – and your good name, if you have one."

A little abashed by his own words Phaeton closed his mouth tight and said nothing more for the moment, until the bearded centaur spoke again.

It took awhile, the centaur chief appraising Phaeton's garments, his sandals, his goat-leather belt.

"I am called Oreus," said the bearded centaur.

"Oreus, I shall tell my divine father of your kindness to me."

"I fear no man," added the centaur.

"The son of my father," retorted Phaeton, impatience and hunger making him feel bold, "fears no man or beast." He added, "I wish to be on my way."

Far to the rear the bald-headed centaur lifted his silver drinking horn and made drinking motions, nothing flowing from the horn.

"Find us wine, young traveler," said Oreus, "and we will see what we can do to aid your journey."

None of the creatures moved aside, except to flail the morning air with their flowing, horselike tails. The centaurs blocked any advance on Phaeton's part, and any retreat, as well, but it was true that as yet they made no move to harm him.

It was then that Phaeton made what he quickly came to realize was a grave mistake.

He lifted his staff and brought it down on the ground before Oreus.

It was not a blow intended to do harm, little more than a loud *thwack.*

Get out of my way, said Phaeton's gesture.

The centaur laughed, and Phaeton made an even worse mistake. He struck the centaur on the forearm – not a serious blow, little more than a warning tap.

The centaur seized the staff, and flung it away. Then he grasped Phaeton by the collar of his tunic, and lifted the youth off his feet.

Phaeton hung suspended, half-choked by the grip that held him high.

The sunny morning changed, then, in an instant.

The trees all around whistled and sighed in a sudden breeze that spun through the treetops, crackled boughs, and fluttered green leaves. The breeze rose yet further, blowing Oreus's long beard.

Just as quickly the wind ceased.

The sudden appearance of a new traveler caught the centaurs' attention. Garbed in a flowing cloak and a broad-brimmed hat that sheltered his features, this arrival carried a long, slender *kerykeion* – a herald's staff. The youth could have been a young woman – both men and women wore the same sort of garments against weather. But his stride was that of an athletic young man, and he gave a gentle chuckle at the sight of Phaeton's predicament.

"*Haie*, Phaeton," called the visitor, a friendly welcome.

The centaurs turned to block the approach of this new presence, and the swiftly arriving traveler laughed aloud.

It was the spirited sound of this laugh that made fear fade within Phaeton, even as he struggled to breathe – Oreus still held him high above the path.

Phaeton's relief continued to grow as the approaching figure stated his business in a clear, pleasing voice, as the best of heralds are expected to do. "I travel on behalf of my masters," he sang out, "who wonder why the son of Apollo has been delayed in his journey."

"This upstart," said Oreus bluntly, hefting Phaeton as he spoke, "shows ill manners."

"Rough manners are not unheard of in the woodland," said the new arrival, stopping before Phaeton. "Even Flora herself is dismayed at your rude ways, Oreus," added the herald with a carefree air. "The goddess of the flowering field is bruised in spirit at the way your hooves tear her blossoms. But does she ask any harm to you, sons of the Ancient Ones? Are you not free to sunder the berry bush and the sage with your careless stampedes?"

The centaurs grew quiet at these words from the youthful figure, and one or two of the muscular steed-men fell back, no longer so bold.

Oreus set Phaeton gently on his feet.

"Flora, goddess of the spring, does us an honor," said Oreus in a changed voice, using formal diction now, "with her untiring patience."

Phaeton was struck wordless by the alteration in the centaur chief. His voice was rough, but his manner was that of dignified apology.

"Entirely right, good centaur," said the herald. "I am pleased that you realize this."

"And every joy we take in brook and field quickens us to life," added the gray-bearded centaur in a cadenced fragment of poetry. He shot a meaningful glance at his fellow creatures.

"In truth," said the youthful centaur, already setting down his round stone beside the path, "we seek no quarrel with any creature."

"Quite so," said the messenger. "I am glad to hear it."

While grateful to be on his feet again, Phaeton was increasingly alarmed.

He had guessed, until now, a good deal less about this new arrival than Oreus and his companions, but the young man's awe was now awakened. The son of Phoebus Apollo knelt on the ground, unwilling to look into the eyes of this very probably divine visitor – perhaps the messenger to the gods himself.

"If my own arrival frightens you, young man," said the herald, his shadow falling over Phaeton, "how will you gather the courage to address your father?"

I will not be able to, Phaeton admitted silently to himself.

I will not be able to speak to him – to the lord of daylight.

He knelt even lower, pressed his forehead against the earth and closed his eyes. Nothing in his learning had prepared him to address such an immortal.

"Words will fail you beyond the edge of the world, Phaeton, will they not?" asked the divine herald.

Speech will die in me, as it has this very moment.

"Stand, Phaeton," said the messenger, touching the traveler's shoulder lightly with his staff, "and let me offer you a warning."

TWELVE

PHAETON STILL could not meet the gaze of the immortal Mercury.

The chastened centaurs were already departing, hurrying off into the woodland, eager to escape the divine presence. A covey of quail burst upward from the herd of horse-men, and the gray-bearded leader raised a hand in apology to the woodland. Such birds are beloved of Diana, goddess of the hunt and of the moon, and the centaurs appeared to be suddenly shy of any disturbance they might cause among the divine powers.

"It is not too late to go home again, Phaeton," said Mercury with a smile.

He wore the appearance of a person younger than Phaeton, and the divine one's eyes were those of a youth without any care. But Phaeton felt the touch of the staff even now, long moments after it had rested for an instant on his shoulder.

His shoulder tingled, and a warmth spread down from that momentary contact, filling Phaeton with strength. His hunger was gone, and so was any trace of weariness.

And yet Phaeton did not trust his voice to speak – not for the moment.

"Already, good Phaeton," said the divine one cheerfully, "you begin to ask yourself, 'have I made a mistake?' Not yet, I can advise you. Not nearly yet. Your mistake, Phaeton, is yet to come."

Phaeton did not want to bring shame to himself, or to his mother – or, indeed, to his homeland – by uttering an awkward remark. But Mercury's statement made the young man uneasy.

The herald seemed to read the young traveler's thoughts.

"Is a mother always wise, Phaeton?" queried the immortal one. "Should a young man always follow a parent's urging?"

Mercury was famous for his telling way with argument, and many philosophers and poets knelt at the crossroads, praying that the divine one might quicken their powers of speech. Phaeton knew that no young man could counter the talents of this immortal, and so he did not try.

"Undying messenger, please grace my journey," prayed Phaeton when he could speak at last.

"Ah," said Mercury, not a syllable so much as a breeze rising from the earth, an upwelling of sadness.

Then he gave a gentle laugh. "You can speak very handsomely, young Phaeton, when you wish to. It's a talent that always wins my heart."

"My divine father will thank you," added Phaeton.

"Have you nothing more to ask me, mortal Phaeton?" asked the herald already cinching his belt and bending to tighten a strap on his gold-leather travel boots, getting ready to depart.

"Is it far to my father's temple?"

"Oh, yes – it's half a world away," said Mercury lightly, as though the message could only please. "Only a divine power could speed you there," he added, squaring his wide-brimmed hat on his head.

Disheartened by this, Phaeton all the more deeply regretted the loss of his supplies. "Why did the water nymph steal my cakes and silver?" asked Phaeton before he could stop himself.

"You owed the nymphs an offering," said Mercury, like someone explaining what was all-too clear, "in return for saving your life."

"When did the nation of nymphs do anything for the son of Clymene?" inquired Phaeton.

Mercury gave another smile. "Did I not hear," he said, "that a dryad kept the bees of a sacred oak from stinging an ardent youth?"

Phaeton had not considered this possibility.

"Run, Phaeton," urged immortal Mercury with a smile, "all the way to the gates of dawn."

Phaeton bounded ahead, but he keenly felt the plodding weight of his progress compared with the leaping strides of the divine messenger.

"Hurry, Phaeton," cheered the youthful-looking god, "you have whole continents to put behind you."

Phaeton lumbered forward, moving as swiftly as he could, it was true, but clumsy alongside the darting herald.

"On the wind, Phaeton," said the messenger.

Phaeton forged ahead, a stitch in his side.

"Like this!" cried the messenger.

He touched the young man's right heel with the tip of his staff.

The deity vanished up the road as Phaeton strode along earnestly, doing as he was told, putting one foot ahead of the other.

Very soon his progress changed.

Berry bushes became a blur.

Winging sparrows and a quick-footed weasel were left far behind. The vixen in her course, the heron in his flight, were all frozen in place, so fleet was Phaeton in his growing joy.

No mortal had ever been so swift.

Spotted deer bounded, and the wild colt, and the gazelle, but Phaeton sprang beyond them all.

He flashed past a cloven-footed satyr spying on women, innocent villagers rinsing clothes beside a river. The satyr jumped, startled as never before, but neither he nor the women glimpsed the youthful son of Apollo as he passed. They were aware only of the explosion into the sky of egrets, startled at the sudden wake that wrinkled the water behind some unseen force, powering east.

Crocodiles stirred in their shallows, and lions looked up from their hiding places, as Phaeton sped across the grassy veldt. The hippopotamus yawning in his pond, the elephant lazing in his water hole, all snorted and rose up, alarmed as the air was split for an instant by a presence approaching, and just as suddenly passed.

So fleet was Phaeton that mountain ranges fell away beneath his feet, and marshland parted.

As the long daylight hours stretched on, and as the sun's chariot swept the high heavens and descended toward sunset, Phaeton sped, snow-splashed peak and mosquito-droning jungle both a blur past the tireless runner.

And still he ran, into the night that rose from the east.

Phaeton's thrill at his wondrous speed was tempered, now, by the knowledge of what he approached.

What will I tell my divine father? wondered Phaeton.

How can I dare to so much as gaze upon him?

And what will I bring myself to say?

If only I could speed like this forever, thought Clymene's son, and never achieve my destination – that would be happiness.

Stars lifted high in the vault of night, and still Phaeton made his way, empowered by Mercury's gift, into the territories far to the east. No mortal had ever wandered into these sun-burnished ridges and heat-blanched valleys before the sun's domain.

The young seeker approached the edge of the world.

THIRTEEN

PHAETON CEASED his onward rush and stood still.

Columns rose up from the darkness, glowing gold and other precious metals pulsing with the subdued but tireless sunlight secreted within. The palace doors were mirrors, displaying the yet-distant figure of the youthful adventurer as he gradually found his courage again and crept forward.

The walls were vast, much higher than any ever built by human hands. Phaeton had heard legends that warned that a mortal could be blinded by the sight of such divine marvels, or perhaps lose his sanity entirely. Phaeton made halting progress forward, step by faltering step, until the young traveler reached out toward his own image, the reflection of an apprehensive youth.

He stretched forth his hand, and touched the image of his own pale, tentative fingers.

The great mirrored gate whispered.

And fell slowly open.

Phaeton hesitated. Perhaps, he thought, it was not too late to turn back.

But he took a step inside.

THREE

FOURTEEN

AT ONCE the young seeker was aware that he was not alone.

A stairway swept upward, toward a nearly blinding presence, a robed figure.

The young man began his faltering climb upward. As swift as he had been all that day, he was halting now, wishing the number of steps could be made countless, so that he might never achieve his goal.

I was a fool, he thought, to attempt such a journey.

Each breath partook of a sweetness like the perfume of the iris, a heady fragrance. This place was at once glorious and disturbing. Once again Phaeton doubted his mother's word. Why would a god from such a temple desire a mortal woman?

As the young man approached the summit of the stairway, a dazzling illumination surrounded him – even when he closed his eyes the light still possessed him.

A voice spoke, as though the palace itself had been gifted with a low, gentle power of speech.

"Why have you come here, Phaeton?" came the question.

Trembling, the young visitor could not speak.

But he did open his eyes.

He knows my name.

The source of the query was a figure in purple, richer than the finest dyer's art, and glittering with points of emerald brilliance. Some said that the gods were much larger than mortals, giants with beautiful features. It was true that Phoebus Apollo was taller than any man Phaeton had ever seen, and heavily muscled, his beard like fine-spun gold.

Above this eminence the vault of a temple rose, in pulsing columns, and Phaeton realized that this citadel, as grand as it was, had been designed to merely echo the handsome presence of its lord.

Yet again the musical voice broke the silence. "My son, why have you come to see me?"

Phaeton let these words slip into his awareness, afraid to give them particular meaning at first.

But the weight of this solemn greeting brought more certainty – and happiness – with each passing heartbeat.

Clymene's son stood straight now, and taking a deep breath allowed his gaze to take in the shapes and colors of this place, a palace Phaeton believed no one of flesh and blood had ever seen before.

Having come so far, and emboldened by the god's question, Phaeton would not be silent now.

FIFTEEN

APOLLO LOVED the sight of any living man or woman.

The lord of light loved the mussel gatherer, with his homely woven basket, and the maiden herding hens with her long, tattered skirt. He loved the bright skein of the fisherman's net, and the song of the wife at work with her wheel and distaff, spinning wool to thread. He adored the laughing comradeship of soldiers, and the songs of children skipping stones across the pond.

When the gambler cursed his luck, or the athlete fell hurt in the gymnasium, Apollo knew it well, and sorrowed with them, because the god of light was in love with every human being.

And the lord of daylight loved his own offspring, more than any other mortals. He loved his human children so greatly that now, as Phaeton made his way up the stairs of the temple of dawn, the god was nearly moved to tears of thanksgiving.

He had other sons and daughters living in the world of mortal men, but even so the sight of Phaeton's youthful strength made his throat swell with joy – and with pride. How keenly he had treasured Clymene, those brief years ago, and how closely Phaeton resembled that mortal beauty, a woman almost as fleet of foot as the spring hare.

The divine one felt a surge of fatherly pride at this visit, and made certain that Days and the Hours – figures like women but surpassing mortal forms with their richly colored gowns – were looking on as his son knelt, trembling still but brave enough to speak.

"Do you call me your son, divine Apollo?" the youth was asking now, his voice as yet breathless.

"I loved your mother, the good-hearted Clymene, and I treasure her still," said the immortal god truthfully. "How do her days pass, Phaeton?" The all-surveying god had been troubled by her absence in recent years, and her habit of clinging to shadows and retreating from his loving eye. "Is she happy?"

Phaeton wished he could choose words with greater mastery. Surely in my ignorance, thought the young seeker, I can only offend this divine being.

"My mother is not as peaceful in her heart," offered Phaeton, rising now from his knees, "as she would be if you acknowledged me as your son."

Phoebus Apollo would have been surprised at this youthful assertiveness, inappropriate in the throne room of an earthly king, and far from fitting the temple of an immortal. He would have been amazed at the foolhardiness of the mortal lad's tone, if he had not recognized his own good-hearted courage in the boy's voice. The sun god had no love of cowardice and hesitation. And he recognized, too, something of Clymene in the lad's bearing.

It was a shame, thought the god of daylight, that these creatures, mortal men and women, would grow old and encounter death's embrace. This insight gave Phoebus Apollo a moment of sharp sorrow, as if the truth were new to the god of light that instant.

"What can I give you, Phaeton?" inquired the god, moved nearly beyond speech by his fatherly affection.

Summer, a figure like a mortal woman enveloped in an aura of auburn hue, put out a hand to Apollo – a gesture of caution – but the lord of light waved her aside. What did any of these eternal ones – Spring with bellflowers in her hair, the Hours, arranged in a patient queue – know about fatherhood? Even Aurora Dawn herself, who stirred the gates of the east to life each day, knew nothing of a parent's love.

Phaeton's eye was alight with wonder at his father's question, and the youth did not speak at once.

"Ask me any favor, Phaeton," encouraged Phoebus Apollo.

"Any favor at all, Father?" asked Phaeton, treasuring the sound of *father* on his breath here in this glowing temple.

"Anything that you might ask is yours, my son," said the sun, "I swear under the heavenly vault of Jupiter."

Phaeton considered this.

The young man saw Epaphus in his mind's eye, one foot on the stricken monster. He heard the young archer's laugh. Phaeton imagined his mother, left for years in shadow, in constant half-dark. He pictured sweet-voiced Ino clearly, and wondered what it would be like to make her think well of him.

"Anything that I ask will be mine?" queried the young man, his voice trembling.

As he spoke he asked himself: what is the one thing that no mortal has ever done before? What single accomplishment will banish all jeers and prove my mother's honor – and my own – for all time?

"Phaeton, why do you doubt me?" said Phoebus Apollo with

a gentle laugh. "I have sworn already, and now I'll go further, and vow that by the deep waters of Hades, on which the gods make their most solemn promises, whatever you wish will be yours."

At these words a figure beyond the Days and the Hours, far to one side of the temple, lifted her eyes in caution. She parted her lips, this lovely presence, seeking words of warning for her lord. She was Century, a silver shape dressed in a gown like woven breath.

"I ask," rang out Phaeton's voice, steady enough now, "to be allowed to drive your chariot – the fiery wheels of the sun – for one entire day across the heavens."

This request shocked Phaeton – no sooner had he been tempted by the desire, than he had put it into words. No doubt the sunny presence of Apollo was responsible for this – the lord of song and poetry was famous for giving encouragement to mortal hopes. And having spoken, Phaeton was determined not to show any of the sickening doubt he was already beginning to feel.

Phoebus Apollo raised a finger to his lips, and turned away.

As the Hours gave a grief-choked chorus of sighs, Apollo began to regret his carefree vow. He felt the first stirrings of misgiving, guessing what disturbed the Hours, murmuring to each other, and what anguish caused the flower-bedecked Spring to bury her face in her hands.

SIXTEEN

FOR A LONG moment Apollo wrapped himself in silence.

Then he gave a laugh, pretending an easy confidence he did not feel.

"What request was that, dear boy?" he asked, as though he could not distinctly recall every word.

"Keep your solemn vow, Father," insisted Phaeton, in his best, most formal language, "one made under the open sky, and let me take the reins of your chariot for a day over the earth."

The immortal shivered inwardly at the sound of this, and yet he gave another hearty laugh, disguising his growing unease.

"Come now, dearest Phaeton," said the lord of daylight, "of all the gifts I could provide for you –"

"This is the one I seek," said Phaeton, before his father could complete his thought. "I claim your word, on your love for my mother."

The sun god kept silent now, mistrusting talk altogether. Argument was prized by mortals, with their love of gossip. The lord of daylight loathed ordinary conversation, and prized poetry and song – words with wings. Apollo realized that he had been foolish to trade speech with his offspring from the world of men.

When he spoke again it was in a new, deeply shaken tone. "Phaeton, what you have asked I cannot give."

Phaeton took a step back, disappointment in his eyes.

"My son, you seek too much," protested the divinity. "You have a mortal's ability, and a young man's skill. Even great Jupiter himself would scarcely be able to control my chariot."

"I see now," said Phaeton, "what my mother discovered years ago – that a god may be quick to promise, but slow to keep his vows."

"The daily course of my own chariot," said Apollo struggling to keep his habitual good temper, "nearly unmans me, Phaeton, the power of the heavenly horse-team is so great."

"It would give my mother well-deserved joy," said the youth, "to see you honor her memory." And it would be proof, Phaeton thought, that your love extends to me.

Phoebus Apollo groaned. "If I could allow you to understand the truth, Phaeton, you would thank me for delivering you from a curse."

"And to think that I have heard my mother praise you," said Phaeton with a quiet bitterness, "telling me often that you were the most generous and bountiful of gods."

"Come with me, my son. Stand at the edge of the earth, beyond the gate," urged Apollo, "and look out at the riches of the hills and valleys. I can give you anything that lightens your gaze."

Phaeton said simply, "I will hold you to your promise."

"It will mean your death," said Phoebus Apollo.

Phaeton gave a bitter smile. The young man was certain that his divine father was exaggerating the danger for reasons of his own. Surely, Phaeton thought, this grand presence could bless my journey with some unknown power, if he wanted to, and ensure my safe return. "So this," said the youth at last, "this is how you honor a loving woman and her son."

Apollo appealed silently to the host of Hours, seeking their counsel. Phoebus Apollo himself – the lord of daylight, who enabled the oracle to foretell both victory and famine – felt stripped of power. His attendants likewise stirred, alarmed but without a word to advise their master.

And then the sun god laughed.

The sound was richer than music, and it quickened the heart of Phaeton as it stilled the anxious pacing of Spring.

Phoebus Apollo was certain that he had solved the riddle of his son's will. "I shall show you the horror you would face, Phaeton," said the divine father, "if you happened to win your wish. The sight will shock you to your senses."

"I'm afraid of nothing," said Phaeton, exaggerating his self-assurance, and yet wishing it were true. He did not want to show his divine father that he was inwardly as weak as any other youth. I must, thought Phaeton, prove myself worthy of Apollo's pride.

"Then we must be fast, Phaeton," his immortal father was saying. "Lucifer, the morning star, begins to dim, and I hear Aurora's footstep, hurrying from place to place, reminding me that daybreak cannot be delayed."

"Where are you taking me, Father?"

"Come along, we have no time," said Apollo, and the son followed across the dawn-streaked grounds of the temple.

SEVENTEEN

"I'LL LET YOU set your hand on fire-breathing Pyrois," Apollo was saying with brisk cheer, "and his companion horses Eous, Aetheon, and Phlegon."

Phaeton could not speak, silenced by the radiant wheels they approached.

This was the golden chariot of legend, and at first Phaeton could not glance at it for more than an instant at a time. The chariot was dazzling, and as the wheels shifted with the impatience of the horses, they gave forth a bone-shaking rumble.

"The steeds of sunlight are already in harness," said the sun god in a voice that did little to disguise his pride in the spirited creatures. "My horses are almost too strong for me on a weary day. Look – they're enough to awaken fear in anyone."

The sounds of the team echoed across the pulsing darkness, hooves resounding, breath thundering, the winged horses already tossing and biting the air, impatient for the touch of their master's whip.

But Phaeton could not spare a glance for these beasts, unable now to tear his attention from the glowing spokes of the chariot.

The frame of the carriage was cunningly crafted of a metal like the purest gold, and the sides of the chariot were formed of shining works of art, smithed from dazzling ore. To see such beauty made Phaeton feel joy – but it frightened him, too. He felt that a mortal youth should not be allowed to see such splendor, and that perhaps the danger this chariot represented was real after all.

And yet he stretched forth a hand, hesitated, and then touched the rim of one of the pulsing wheels.

It was warm, and vibrated under his hand. Feeling this power – an entire carriage simmering with the power of daylight – Phaeton wanted to master it. He was impatient to set off, without a further word.

"Vulcan, the divine artist, crafted her," said Apollo, his voice husky with affection for his son – and pride in the chariot. "No work of art is so fine, under the dome of heaven."

Phaeton barely heard his father's words, thinking only that Epaphus would not dare jeer at the sight of the bright wheels. His rival would not laugh – not when the archer beheld Phaeton at the reins of this legendary chariot.

The air shook as horses struck sparks with their hooves, nickered and thundered, eager to fly, as Phoebus Apollo laughed again. "You are right to look so alarmed, dear Phaeton. But hurry – we must be quick. Run your hand along Pyrois and see how uncontrollable he is."

But Phaeton disregarded his father's prompting and stepped up, into the chariot. The well-balanced carriage shifted only very slightly with the young man's weight, and the reins were so heavy that at first he could not heft them.

The iridescent horses tossed their bright manes, their nostrils flaring with excitement, and Pyrois, the leader, looked back over the traces to see what novice groped the reins. The scent of these creatures, fed on ambrosia, was sweet, and their eyes sky-blue. The team mock-battled one another, arching their necks and biting the air, and only Apollo's touch on the harness kept the chariot from vaulting off.

Phaeton felt the wheels continue to grind and tremble, and

the reins he parted at last shifted like living things in his hands. He was dumb with wonder – but his heart quickened, too, with an increasing confidence.

If I can climb the sky-filling Nymph Tree seeking a gift of honey, he told himself, and if I can find my way to the temple of the sun, surely with a little effort I can master such a carriage.

Apollo lifted a hand and hooked a finger under the bridle of Pyrois. At a whisper from their master the horses grew calmer, and the sun god said, "You see, my son, how no touch but mine can command them."

"I can do this, father, you'll see," said Phaeton, his voice rough with feeling. "I will make you proud of me."

Apollo ran his hands over Pyrois's fetlocks and hooves, studying the horseshoes long ago fashioned by Vulcan, the divine, moody artist whose skill sometimes amazed even the gods. Apollo took a long moment to consider Phaeton's words.

Why am I so troubled? the sun god silently inquired of the air around him.

"When has any doubt ever chained my spirit?" said Apollo aloud. "Why don't I choose hope, that ever-returning faith in things to come?"

Pyrois snorted, a rumble like a mountain heaving.

Apollo loved the look of eagerness and joy in Phaeton's eye.

Mortals and gods alike, the god thought, will say: *See how brave young Phaeton is – he is every bit his father's son.*

Apollo smiled.

"I'll cover your face with balm," said the lord of daylight with growing excitement, "to keep your cheeks from blistering."

Phaeton held the reins in both hands, recalling all that he had learned of horses, too delighted – and anxious – to trust his voice.

"Phaeton," the god said, smiling, "they'll remember this day as long as there is poetry and song."

He laughed again and was lost in a brief vision of triumph, great Jupiter admiring Apollo's human son.

"Ah, Phaeton," sighed the god, "you'll win honor for us both."

EIGHTEEN

PHAETON'S FATHER anointed his son's face with balm from a *pyxis* – a small medicine box.

The balm smelled sweeter than the oil of nard Clymene kept, a gift from her mortal husband. Phoebus Apollo's fingers were gentle as they soothed the protective oil across Phaeton's cheeks and forehead.

"Now you'll be able to brave the heat, my son," said Apollo with a smile.

Phaeton smiled in return, struck by the care and affection of his father.

But all the while the horses tossed their manes, Pyrois storming in his harness, eyes wild again. Now the steeds sliced the air with their wings, kept from leaping into the heavens only by Apollo's sudden grasp on the side of the carriage. The sun-god used all his might to steady the team as the wheels fought forward and back.

The reins sank deeper into Phaeton's grasp, just as the sound of an ironlike echo ripped the fading dark.

The sound of this metallic crash, above all else, dented Phaeton's confidence.

The young man took a firmer stance against the jostling of the chariot as it trembled, nearly a living thing, and he could not keep from asking with his eyes, *Father, what was that?*

"That rumbling sound, Phaeton," said the god of the sun, his smile fading, "is the barrier between night and day falling open. Tethys herself, mother of the rivers and sister of the ocean, lets the gate fall at the end of every night."

The young man was too troubled by the weight of the reins in his hands to ask further. They had already drained his arms of strength, but at the same time the reins felt alive, wrestling and twisting in his grip as the horses struggled to set forth. Even so the sound of this ancient name awakened further awe in the youth.

And uttering the name of such a timeless being brought a new sobriety to the god. "Do you insist on fulfilling your desire, Phaeton," inquired Apollo, "despite all that you see and hear?"

"I will do this, Father," Phaeton barely managed to say. He was no longer so confident, but all the more determined.

The immortal nodded, still hopeful of honor, but weighed down by the knowledge he struggled to put into words, the god of prophecy and epic shaken with renewed doubt. "Then follow the ruts worn in the sky-road, my son – the marks the wheels have left from all the other circuits I have taken."

"I will," managed Phaeton, his jaw clenched.

"Skirt the southern reaches of heaven and avoid the far north," continued Apollo. "You can master this, if you put your will into it," counseled the immortal one, as though trying to convince himself. "Ride the middle road. You'll have to avoid the writhing serpent on the right hand, and struggle to avoid the great scorpion on your left. Fortune guide you, my son! And never touch the whip."

"Never!" Phaeton agreed.

The god touched young Phaeton's arm, the divine grasp enclosing the youthful strength of his offspring. His warm touch made Phaeton's vision all the brighter, his pulse even stronger.

"You will bear no shame, Phaeton," said the lord of daylight, "if you relent and watch me set forth, illuminating seas and mountains just as every day before." The god spoke with feeling, already hungering for the vista of the spreading earth and all the lively creatures he loved so well.

The reins glowed with an increasing light, dawn flooding the darkness.

"Father, I thank you," said Phaeton formally, remembering the courtesy he had learned in Merops's home.

His son's speech was not poetry, but it was deeply felt. Touched by these words of gratitude, the lord of daylight stepped back and readied his farewell.

But the act of removing his hand from the rim of the chariot lightened its weight.

The winged steeds leaped forward.

The way was open, and the temple of the sun rocked and fell away behind the youth, the reins at once snaking from his grasp.

NINETEEN

PHAETON GATHERED the streaming reins with great effort, and pulled back on the surging team, just as he had seen chariot drivers do on racing days in his boyhood – it now seemed so long ago.

The wheels radiated heat, and the reins grew even warmer. The team sensed the young man's strain, and Pyrois looked back, taking in the sight of the sweating youth. The team leaped higher, the chariot lighter than ever before, the temple of the sun far behind – far beyond the spinning clouds.

Too high.

They were already far too lofty, the early morning light descending from the glowing wheels of the chariot, land and ocean dropping away below. The heat from the churning, bounding wheels made Phaeton cringe and crouch, as far down as he could in the safety of the chariot while the horses escaped their usual course. Those powerful creatures, used to the burden and touch of a god, were liberated by the feel of a nearly empty carriage.

Far north they fled, celebrating their freedom – but half-panicked, too. Toward the frigid polar limits they climbed, the ice below glowing for the first hour since time began, frozen seas reflecting the spinning brilliance of the spoked and fiery wheels.

It could have been a moment, or it could have been an hour, as the shock of the chariot's heat steamed the frozen waste. White-pelted bears dived into the seas, the water in turmoil under the sudden flood of ice-melt. Avalanches tumbled down the face of virgin mountains, glaciers heaving into pieces, icebergs cascading. The tusked walrus floundered, simmering in brine.

The serpent that hides in the northern vasts, the legendary sullen giant, awoke, singed and angry, his scales blistering. The fanged head lifted from its cavern, seeking upward, wanting to strike this blinding source of danger.

The team of horses sensed the uncoiling menace and winged higher. Phaeton gathered his courage and stood erect again, leaning back with all his power, pulling on the reins to no effect as he prepared to look down to find the proper course, the route they had abandoned.

Not yet.

I'll look down in a moment.

Bracing his spirits, he leaned over the side of the chariot, and the steaming, cooking abyss of the northern ice rose up to meet his gaze, the fabled serpent writhing, turning away defeated by the heat, seeking refuge in the earth.

Phaeton recalled a youth impatient with his gentle stepfather, and the meaningless mockery of a foolish archer.

Now Phaeton wished he had not so much as glimpsed his divine father's horses, and he longed to be nothing more than a daydreamer again, taking his ease beside his stepfather's fountain.

The team of coursers fled south across the heavens, heedless of the chariot they trailed. They rampaged far across the sky, ever higher, further south, until the figures of the zodiac began to stir, the ram and the fabled bull startled into life.

Before Phaeton could cry out, the scorpion itself twitched its tail and stretched its weapon far, the point of the fabled stinger reaching, striking, and striking again.

Almost spearing Phaeton.

The reins fled the young man's grasp, and the team plunged.

FOUR

TWENTY

CYCNUS WOKE.

It was still dark, that weakening, silvered darkness that so often appeared just before dawn, an hour Phaeton's young cousin had never liked.

He loved night well enough, especially in the rain, a storm whispering over the roof. He enjoyed early evening, family gathered to enjoy watered wine and sing songs of ancient heroes. But best of all he preferred daylight, Cycnus and Phaeton pretending they were battling giants under the wide blue, or putting on mock sea battles, a meadow transformed by their imagination into a rolling sea.

An owl broke off one of her sharp cries, and in the roof overhead Cycnus heard the soft, brief scrabble of talons as the flying hunter returned. Some people said that the owl was beloved of the goddess Minerva, and Cycnus believed it must be true.

"Wise goddess, keep my cousin safe," prayed Cycnus.

Phaeton had always chuckled at Cycnus for believing that the eagle belonged to Jupiter, and the peacock to his consort Juno, but Cycnus took such matters seriously. When local villagers took the trouble to feed a leaf to a passing tortoise – believing that the slow-moving creatures brought good luck – Cycnus joined in, offering the lowly creature fresh slices of apple.

Phaeton's cousin rose from his pallet bed and padded out into the hallway, shivering in his nightshirt. Someone in the courtyard was carrying an oil lamp, the flame trembling, one of the servants setting forth braziers of glowing coals against the predawn chill.

Lampetia and Phaethusa were whispering somewhere, already awake and dressed by the sound of it, and the sound of their voices made Cycnus fade back again to his bed chamber.

Cycnus pulled the blanket over his shoulders against the cool air.

How long can the dark continue? he wondered.

Surely it should be morning by now.

Clymene was awake just as dawn chased the stars from the sky.

The ascending light of day, on this particular morning, was somewhat slow to follow. Birds stirred, sang, and then settled once again, as shadows that had begun to lift deepened once more.

Clymene had been unable to sleep for hours, feeling the weight of Phaeton's absence with every heartbeat. She had breathed a prayer to Juno, queen of the gods and wife to Jupiter – she was the goddess most likely to attend to the cares of a mother.

But hers was merely a spoken prayer. A prayer to Juno not accompanied by a gift of *pthois* – sweetened sacrificial cake – or a pitcher of wine for the temple attendants, was unlikely to win much notice from such a sovereign immortal.

Nonetheless Phaeton's mother concluded her devotions, "Bring him back safe to me, my only son."

And soon.

Do not let him complete his journey.

TWENTY-ONE

HER DAUGHTERS were awake, too, Clymene saw as she slipped into the courtyard.

"Hail, Mother, and the gods' blessing on us all," recited Lampetia.

This was not simple rote courtesy. It would not be wise to begin a day without showing respect to both one's parents and the gods.

"You'll be cold, both of you," said Clymene. "You should be wearing something warm."

"We couldn't sleep, Mother," said Lampetia. "Phaethusa had a dream."

They were garbed in lightly woven linen chitons, and the morning was chilly, dew dappling the courtyard bricks at their feet. They warmed their hands over a container of coals one of the servants looked after even now, stirring the embers to new heat.

"It's almost as though winter has come back again," said Clymene, running her hands over her arms. She did not want to hear about another of Phaethusa's nightmares. Her eldest daughter was a big-eyed, silent young woman, with wild and haunted dreams.

"Or as if the sun is late in rising," agreed Lampetia, absent-mindedly.

Lampetia held the griffin feather brought back by Phaeton, and cradled it in her hand.

"I'm sure Phaeton found a nice inn, with a soft pillow to rest his weary head," she said at last.

Comfortable inns were not unheard of, Clymene knew, and it was considered bad luck to mistreat a traveler, especially a young man of position. But much more common were the lowly taverns, rough places if not unsafe, with bad wine sold for a shrewd price, and bugs in the ticking.

"And a dish of smoked fish to go with his honey-figs," agreed Phaethusa, naming one of Phaeton's favorite meals.

Clymene had to laugh. Both of her daughters spoke with a forced confidence – Clymene was touched by this. She kissed Lampetia, and Phaethusa, too. Perhaps Phaeton had heard a night-bird lifting a tune of longing and felt homesick – after one short night. Perhaps he was already on his way back to his family. It was possible, if the gods so willed it.

"I dreamed," said Phaethusa, "that Phaeton was swimming in a river."

This certainly did not sound like a nightmare, thought Clymene. Perhaps the dream foretold some wonderful event.

"He saw me," continued Phaethusa, "and called out –"

Before Phaethusa could finish telling her dream, a sound interrupted her – a pulsing flutter, from high above.

Scattered leaves did a wild dance as a gust of wind blew over the roof tiles, and spun around the fountain, followed by an even greater wind, a warm, dry gale from the east that blew a speck of grit into Clymene's eye. The wind trailed off into a stillness, and silence fell over the countryside.

But the silence was not perfect.

From far off came the sound of cries, far and wide – the startled calls of farmland fowl, geese and crows, and the birds of the wild, the swallow and the hawk.

"Whatever can be wrong?" asked Lampetia, shading her eyes against the sky.

TWENTY-TWO

BIRDS SWARMED AND TUMBLED.

Entire flocks – tribes, nations – of the feathered creatures formed tossing clouds overhead as the sunlight swelled, its withering heat driving the blue from the sky.

And then the sunlight just as quickly began to fade. Shadows swelled again as the daylight began a flight to the north. Birds poured from the sky, seeking refuge in brush and wood, some of them smoking, too late to hide, already singed and heat-stunned.

Just as suddenly the sun careened away from the north. Clymene hurried to the fountain and stood on her tiptoes, straining to see the morning light over walls of the villa. And then she could observe it easily, the familiar orb of the divine chariot as it wheeled across heaven.

Only to lose its way again, and tumble southward – or was it falling to earth? Far off a human being let out a wail, and another wind – hotter than Vulcan's fire – emptied over the land.

If such a thing were possible, thought Clymene.

If such a thing could happen, she thought, half-guessing and sickened at her private fear.

Pigs screamed in distant farmyards, a sound like human terror.

But such a calamity was not possible, Phaeton's mother reminded herself. Her knees were weak, and her speech failed, but she repeated this certainty to herself: this could not be what it seemed.

She hurried down the hall, past the busts of Merops's ancestors, followed by the rapid footsteps of her husband, his chiton thrown on quickly, hanging unevenly as he ran, joining his wife in the village street. His entire household shielded their eyes against the errant, staggering sunlight.

A bull broke from its pen and ran, lowing in panic through the village. The street was crowded with half-clad villagers, smiths and clerks, plowwrights and slaves, all wild-eyed and disheveled.

Epaphus arrived in the street clinging to his bow, the young hunter leading white-haired Aristander by one arm. The old veteran had fallen, momentarily blinded by the sunlight – and now the wooden roof of his smithy was alight.

"What have we done," cried Aristander, "to offend the gods?"

Epaphus could say nothing, frightened and wide-eyed, but others joined the veteran in an outcry directed at the sky, toward the divine ones.

Ino and her mother joined the throng, baffled and afraid.

"Hurry, everyone – come into my house," called Merops, pulling in his neighbors, pushing them into the security of his stout-walled home.

But Clymene did not follow.

At that moment blond-haired Cycnus joined her, squinting, one hand blocking the ever-shifting sun.

Shielding her eyes against the errant, blinding source of light she called for Phoebus Apollo.

When the sky seemed deaf except for the shrieks of a few surviving birds, fuming and in flames as they plummeted from the sky, Clymene raised her voice, calling for cloud-gathering Jupiter himself to come to the aid of earth.

And to save her son.

TWENTY-THREE

THE CHARIOT glowed white-hot beneath Phaeton's feet.

The youth held on to the edge of the carriage, the reins streaming uncontrollably around and over him.

He made no further attempt to master the fiery team as the soles of his leather travel boots burned and his flesh blistered.

In his despair he remembered the passions and hopes of a young man scalded by taunts, questioning his loving mother, leaving behind a caring stepfather. In his mind Phaeton could see the image of a youth, who spared too little time for lively Cycnus, loyal cousin and friend.

The winged team of coursers swept upward, to the heaven's summit, where the air was thin and Phaeton's breath came in painful gasps. The horses climbed, only to dive downward again, fiery manes flowing, as meadows burst into flame at the chariot's approach.

Wild bison stampeded, their hides smoldering, and the silver-feathered owl, blinded by all-consuming day, caught fire in flight. The alder trees burst into leaves of flame, and sacred springs began to simmer and boil dry.

Fear-sick, Phaeton could not shape a further prayer. He clung hard to keep from tumbling from the chariot as he thought he heard the anguish of farmers and villagers, stricken mortals far below.

Forests smoked and gave way to flame, and volcanoes smoldered from outside as well as within. When he had summoned his courage Phaeton struggled upward, holding tight to the chariot's edge, and looked down to see the spreading riot of fire in the chariot's wake. Where forest had cloaked the hilltops, new desert broke, an expanse of bare bedrock.

Nymphs bewailed the loss of springs, as sands along the rivers melted into glass and currents boiled, steaming entirely away. Whooping cranes burned, casting feathered embers from their wings, and seas withered, retreating, leaving barren earth. The tuna cooked in his shrinking abyss, whales searching out the depths and dying.

Not even Neptune, god of the teeming sea, could bear to gaze skyward, blanched by the light from above.

Phaeton keened yet another prayer.

Immortal father, great Jupiter, bring an end to this.

TWENTY-FOUR

JUPITER LOVED QUIET.

The open blue, the burgeoning cloud, rain-freshened dawns, and deep sunsets – these were the sky god's great pleasures, and the everlasting chill of high places was his eternal joy.

That morning the cloud-gathering god was in his highest temple. Juno his wife had just left his presence that early hour, after arguing long and well that a favorite creature of hers deserved a boon.

Now Jupiter was glad to be alone with his own thoughts.

He loved the song of rain freshening new-plowed farmland. He liked calm and logic. Too much talk wearied him at times. He stood now at the far end of his temple and drank in the cool, sweet freshness all around.

Perfect peace was rare, even here among the divine. Mount Olympus, the dwelling place of the gods, was so often in tumult. Mars and Minerva frequently argued with each other, and the powerfully built, half-lame Vulcan was always arriving with some new device of genius – a bowl of gold as big as a lake bed, or a newly fashioned archery set for Diana, even though the weapons she possessed were already beautiful enough.

This morning violet-eyed Juno had asserted that the goose deserved more respect. The goddess had always praised the peacock, with its spreading plumes, and Jupiter could certainly understand that. But why, of all creatures, did Juno now sing the praises of that rude, long-necked fowl?

Well, what did it matter? reflected the great god with a chuckle. Minerva, the goddess of wisdom, had her own temples and honorable owl. Mars, bringer of war, had his monuments and his bright-feathered woodpecker. Jupiter admired fairness, in himself and others, and he was generous by nature. He would ask Mercury to shape a decree. A sacred flock of geese would grace the beautiful temple of Juno, and be honored as a sacred bird.

Even a god can be surprised. As Jupiter was just then, when a figure hurried across the temple grounds, and splashed so swiftly over the broad pools that the footsteps of the herald carried across the water.

The youthful-looking messenger swept the broad-brimmed hat from his head and knelt.

"Rise up, Mercury," said the gentle-voiced Jupiter. He liked this herald very much, and always felt his heart lighten at the quick-footed immortal's approach. "What troubles you this morning?"

If, in fact, it *was* morning, Jupiter thought just then. Sunny cool had turned to even colder twilight in an instant, mountain shadows stretching and then shrinking away as the sunlight came and went unsteadily.

"I cannot bring myself to tell you, lord of all," said the herald.

The messenger's usual lively tones were muted.

"You will," said Jupiter simply. "Please, good Mercury," the immortal father added, kind-hearted even then, and increasingly puzzled at the behavior of the daylight beyond the temple.

"The tidings are too grim," said the messenger.

Jupiter nearly laughed. "Nothing can be so dreadful, herald. Unless, perhaps, an angry goose has attacked some brave warrior – and pinched him to death."

"The children, my lord Jupiter," Mercury began. "The boys and girls of mortal men and women –"

"What of them?" interrupted the sky god with a darkening frown. He nearly felt like telling the herald to wait for a moment, for beyond the columns of the temple the sunlight was suddenly impossibly bright.

"I fear to voice my tidings," said Mercury in the finest herald speech, "without a promise from the father of all –"

"Wise herald," said Jupiter with some impatience, "I will not hold you responsible for your news, good or bad."

"Earth is burning," said the herald in a burst, anguish in his voice. "Men and women, and their children, cry to you for help."

Jupiter looked away, and briefly weighed these tidings. "Herald," he said, "this cannot be true."

But Mercury's gaze was steady, his youthful-looking features set in an expression of sorrow. And Jupiter groaned, realizing then the meaning of the distant, panicked cries of birds.

"Tell me, loyal Mercury," Jupiter said at last, the gentleness of his tone giving the greater weight to his question. "Who has done this?"

TWENTY-FIVE

PHAETON CLUNG to the edge of the chariot.

The horses surged in terror from star to forest, from moon to ocean floor.

The youth was certain that this day would not end, and that his prayer remained unheard by the immortals. His voice torn, he lifted a final plea at last to Mercury, the divine messenger, repeating a fragment of the old song, *quicken my prayer.*

Divine Mercury, do not forget me.

Jupiter strode to the ridge from which, in the long, peaceful mornings, he so often surveyed the spreading patchwork of the world.

He had been hoping, despite his growing unease, that Mercury had been mistaken. The herald had a gift for vivid description – surely matters could not be as bleak as he asserted.

Jupiter was stunned.

The chief of the gods was shaken to his heart by what he saw, and touched by the cries and prayers that rose up to him from the world of mortals.

And the god was appalled at the sight of the pitching, careening chariot, a blazing streak of sunlight.

Jupiter had long admired Phoebus Apollo's wheeled carriage. Many days, while divine bickering echoed throughout Olympus, Jupiter had often thought *how wonderful to do nothing but ride across the sky.*

And how splendid to mingle with beautiful mortals. Jupiter had an eye for mortal women, himself, and would have enjoyed more opportunity to seek their company. That would be an additional benefit of being the sun god – spying women from on high, as they bathed and wandered. Phoebus Apollo had for ages been able to pick out the comely and sweet-natured, and Jupiter had envied him.

"Bring me the god of the sun," growled Jupiter.

"As you wish, my lord," said Mercury.

The herald settled the wide-brimmed hat on his head – but he did not leave at once.

"You will, perhaps, spare young Phaeton's life," suggested Mercury.

Jupiter's answer was a scowl.

Slow to anger though he might be, he had faith in justice. And the lord of sky was angry, too, at himself – that he had not sensed this calamity before this moment, lost in his own thoughts.

The chief of the gods flexed his fingers. He lifted his fist and sent a flash, a javelin of blue lightning, toward the chariot of the sun as it ascended again, horses shrieking as Phaeton reeled.

One moment the son of Phoebus Apollo braced himself for another lunge of the chariot. Soon, he knew, the chariot would rise so high he would grow senseless from the thin air and fall. Nothing could spare the earth from harm, he knew – it was too late.

The chariot was at its highest point that seemingly endless morning when Phaeton heard it coming, for an instant, that crackling blue streak. And perhaps he guessed what had happened, mortal prayers being heard at last. But before he could experience any sensation of relief the whipcrack of light sent young Phaeton tumbling, his hair alight. There was a moment of agony and confusion, fire streaming from his eyes.

Then Phaeton's memory fled, and along with it all of his fear.

The young seeker knew nothing more.

The spokes of the chariot rained far, scattering, a burning shower. Cowherds and ferrymen alike beheld the distant blaze arc across the sky, Phaeton streaking from above.

Clymene, watching from her fountain-splashed courtyard, saw this meteor, too, and in some shadowy corner of her heart began to guess what it was.

The horses of the sun broke free of the flaming traces and escaped toward the corners of the world. Until at last the flaming remains of Phaeton burned their way downward, spinning into the deep waters of the River Eridanus.

The current seethed briefly, and closed over his ashes. With a long moan, the wide earth settled and was still.

A smoldering, stunned peace fell over the land, blessed by the loving eye of Jupiter, who gave his gentle rains to woodland torn by fires, and his cooling breath to parched fields.

Naiads stirred in the eddying river.

They crept through the deep, seeking Phaeton's resting place.

TWENTY-SIX

THESE NYMPHS swam downward, gathering Phaeton's broken, charred remains as creatures stole from their hiding places – the egret and the crocodile, the fisherman and the tiger. A soothing wind combed through the charred reeds, and a mist like a balm drifted from heaven.

As joyous in their relief as these graceful water nymphs were, they felt a particular sorrow. They mourned a young man eager to discover the temple of his father. And they had heard of the sport that one of their kind had enjoyed at the young seeker's expense, a stolen pack of fruit and silver.

These naiads of the west gathered now and lay the fragments of young Phaeton on the river bank.

They lifted a song,

Sun and moon,
earth and sea,
which of you have climbed
higher than shining Phaeton?

The nymphs buried the ashes of the son of Phoebus, and carved the words of their song on the stone over his remains.

The sound of the naiads' song rippled through the greening leaves from island to shore.

It whispered across the freshening fields of wheat, carried by Zephyr, the west wind.

TWENTY-SEVEN

FOR ONE long day after Phaeton's fall the sun did not rise.

Some say Jupiter himself had to undertake the task of consoling bereft Phoebus Apollo.

The lord of daylight did not want to see his winged steeds again, nor ride the wide sky. Only the chief of the gods could encourage the brokenhearted father of Phaeton. The stories are told of the fiery, winged horses returning spent and weary to their stables from the widespread dark.

One entire day the sun did not rise, that day a long and seamless night, and some mortals later swore that they heard Vulcan's hammer, forging a new chariot high above the plains and valleys in the mountainous refuge of Olympus.

Clymene and her daughters heard the murmur of the naiads' song in the soft wind.

"Surely he's still alive," said Lampetia.

"Phaeton is waiting for us!" insisted Cycnus, the loyal cousin.

Clymene said much less, warned by the glance of Phaethusa.

Clymene's eldest daughter had seen Phaeton in her sleep before the fiery dawn had broken, and had heard her brother's warning in a dream that she had whispered at last into her mother's ear.

I am lost,
but wait for you.

Perhaps this dream was Juno's way of answering a mother's prayer. There was no mistaking the sad message. Clymene and her daughters, joined by Cycnus, boarded a ship and sailed downriver to the sea, and had the sailors set the sails for western waters.

As the sunlight resumed its circuit, the ocean swells glittering, seabirds gliding once again, Clymene sensed the sun's somber course, the hours passing slowly, the sunlight not quick to chase the morning mist.

The ship sailed westward.

Cycnus saw them first – the beckoning arms in the mouth of the river, the glowing faces of the naiads.

And he heard their voices, half-spoken, half-conveyed by thought, *Here.*

Phaeton is here.

TWENTY-EIGHT

MOTHER, DAUGHTERS, and cousin all hurried through the bulrushes along the shore, only to stop at the sight of Phaeton's grave, the nymph-carved lettering visible in the limestone surface.

"This can't be true!" protested Cycnus.

"What have they done with brave Phaeton?" asked Lampetia, bewildered.

Phaethusa, with her steady gaze, began an ancient, heartfelt song, a hymn of mourning.

"Any song but that," beseeched Cycnus, the youthful cousin certain that he would some day see Phaeton alive once more.

Clymene joined in, the words quieting the river, and stirring the naiads to rise from the water's depths.

One hour, three,
our starlight on the tide,
too brief.

Lampetia was too sorrow-struck to sing this time-honored song.

She raised her arms to heaven. As she shook her fists in sorrow and anger, her hands trembled in the sunlight. Her fingers started into leaves and her arms snaked into branches.

"Mother, help me!" gasped Clymene's youngest daughter.

Her feet speared twin roots down into the soil.

Phaethusa, too, sang with such grief that her voice was enclosed by the sinuous branches of a tree, her hair twisting – belly, womb, and heart all turned to wood as her song ebbed.

Clymene ran from one daughter to another, embracing them, their pulses dimming into solid pith.

Divine Phoebus Apollo loved poetry and song, and delighted in cunning tales of love and victory. Perhaps this power, and his musical voice, had won Clymene's heart, all those years ago.

Now Clymene was finished with poetry and music, but she would love her son forever, in silence.

By the grave of Phaeton a third tree stretched its branches, Clymene's leaves shining in the sun.

Cycnus wandered the shore, his grief so fierce that he, too, could not make a sound. Some say his sorrow moved the naiads to raise a prayer to the immortals to alter his shape. Some say that Cycnus's mourning alone wrought the profound change from youth to waterfowl.

Gliding in his own reflection, at last a cygnet was all that remained of Phaeton's cousin, graceful and long-necked, the male swan brilliant white in the afternoon sun. To this day the swan glides in quiet waters, remembering a cousin who had climbed far.

TWENTY-NINE

ONE MORNING a soft footstep stirred the grasses, and the shadow of a broad-brimmed hat and a herald's staff fell upon Phaeton's resting place among the trees.

"*Haie*, Phaeton," said divine Mercury – not sadly, but as a young man greeting a friend.

The divine herald cocked his head and listened to the silence all around.

"I have not forgotten you, young seeker," said the immortal messenger.

He stretched forth his staff and touched the earth.

A long sigh, a breeze rising from the earth, swept through the leaves of the three spreading trees, swirling upward, the soul of a young traveler escaping darkness.

Phaeton felt life again, stretching his limbs. But even as he joyed in the sensation of sunlight, he knew that he was no longer one of the mortals.

"Run, Phaeton," said immortal Mercury. Or perhaps he uttered an unspoken urging.

Forever speed the earth.

Now when mortals run fast, sprinting under the sky, they are joined by the son of divine Apollo and his beloved Clymene.

The wind is Phaeton's breath.

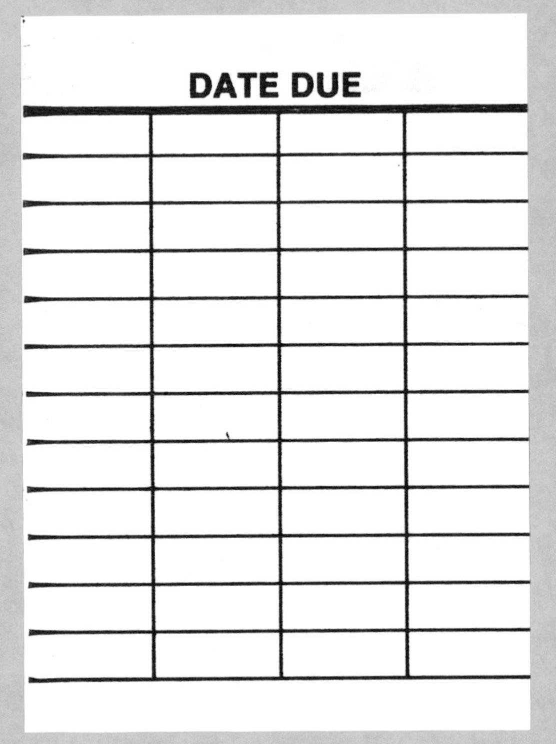
DATE DUE